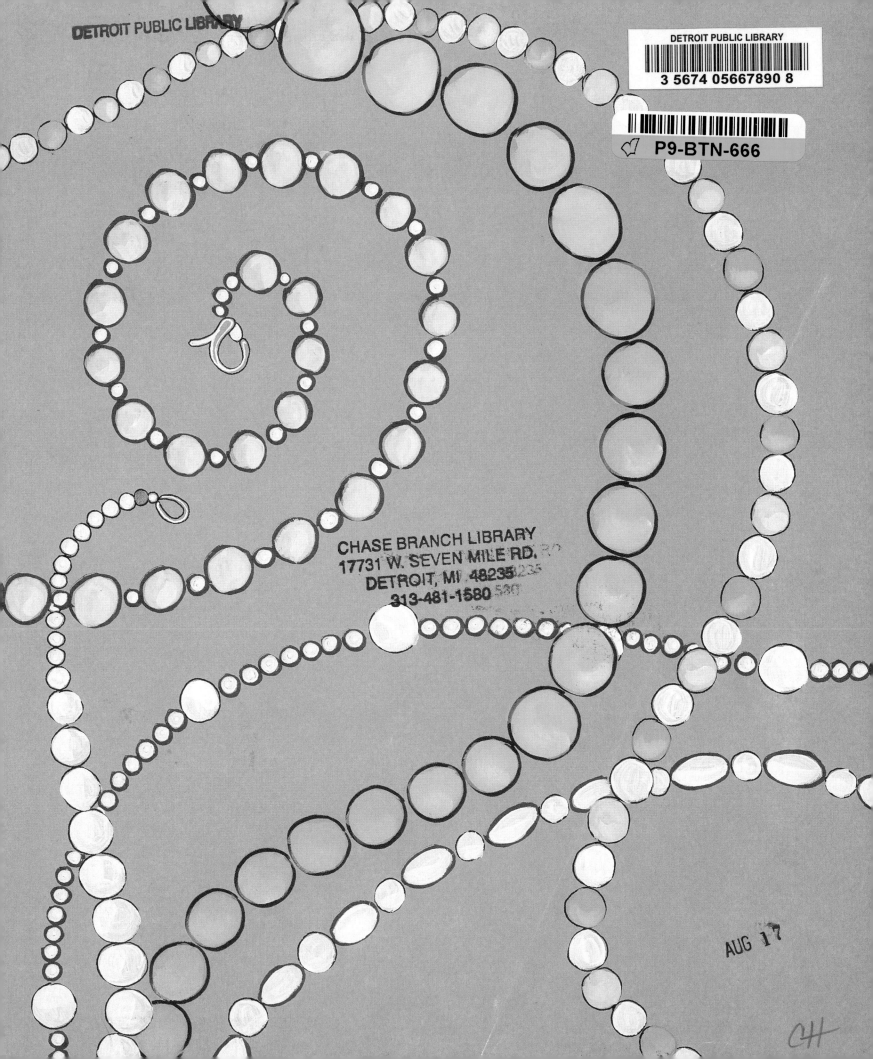

Carolrhoda Books
A division of Lerner Publishing Group, Inc.
241 First Avenue North
Minneapolis, MN 55401 USA

For reading levels and more information, look up this title at www.lernerbooks.com.

Main body text set in Aroma LT Pro Regular.
Typeface provided by Linotype AG.

The images in this book are used with the permission of: Portrait image courtesy Elizabeth Zunon; © Everett
Collection Inc/Alamy, p. 26 (top); courtesy of Vaunda Micheaux Nelson, p. 26 (middle right); © Robert Abbott
Sengstacke/Getty Images, p. 26 (middle left); © Everett Collection Historical/Alamy, p. 26 (bottom); © Robert
Abbott Sengstacke/Getty Images, p. 27 (top); © Julieta Cervantes/The New York Times/Redux, p. 27 (bottom).

Library of Congress Cataloging-in-Publication Data

Nelson, Vaunda Micheaux, author.
    Don't call me grandma / by Vaunda Micheaux Nelson ; illustrated by Elizabeth Zunon.
      pages   cm
    Summary: A granddaughter recounts the reasons why her grandmother is hard to love—and why she
loves her anyway.
    ISBN: 978-1-4677-4208-5 (lib. bdg. : alk. paper)
    ISBN: 978-1-4677-9559-3 (EB pdf)
    1. Grandmothers—Juvenile fiction. 2. Old age—Juvenile fiction. [1. Grandmothers—Fiction. 2. Old
age—Fiction. 3. African Americans—Fiction.] I. Zunon, Elizabeth, illustrator. II. Title.

PZ7.N43773Gr 2016
[E]—dc23   2014030585

Manufactured in the United States of America
1 – DP – 12/31/15

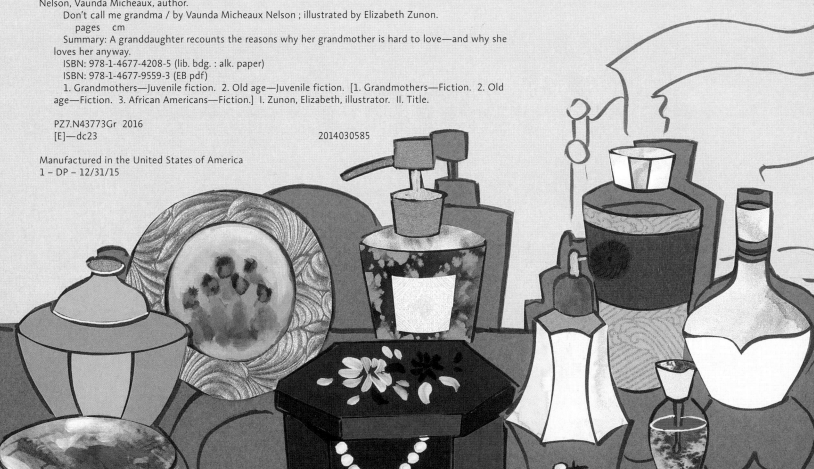

Don't Call Me Grandma

Vaunda Micheaux Nelson

illustrations by Elizabeth Zunon

Carolrhoda Books • Minneapolis

Great-Grandmother Nell is scary.
Once I forgot and called her
"Grandma." She yanked my ear,
leaned in close, and said, "It's
grandMOTHER, my pretty,"
just like the witch in *The
Wizard of Oz*.

Great-Grandmother Nell fries fish and boils grits for breakfast.

I like fish, but for breakfast? And with the heads on and the creepy fish eye looking right at me from my plate?

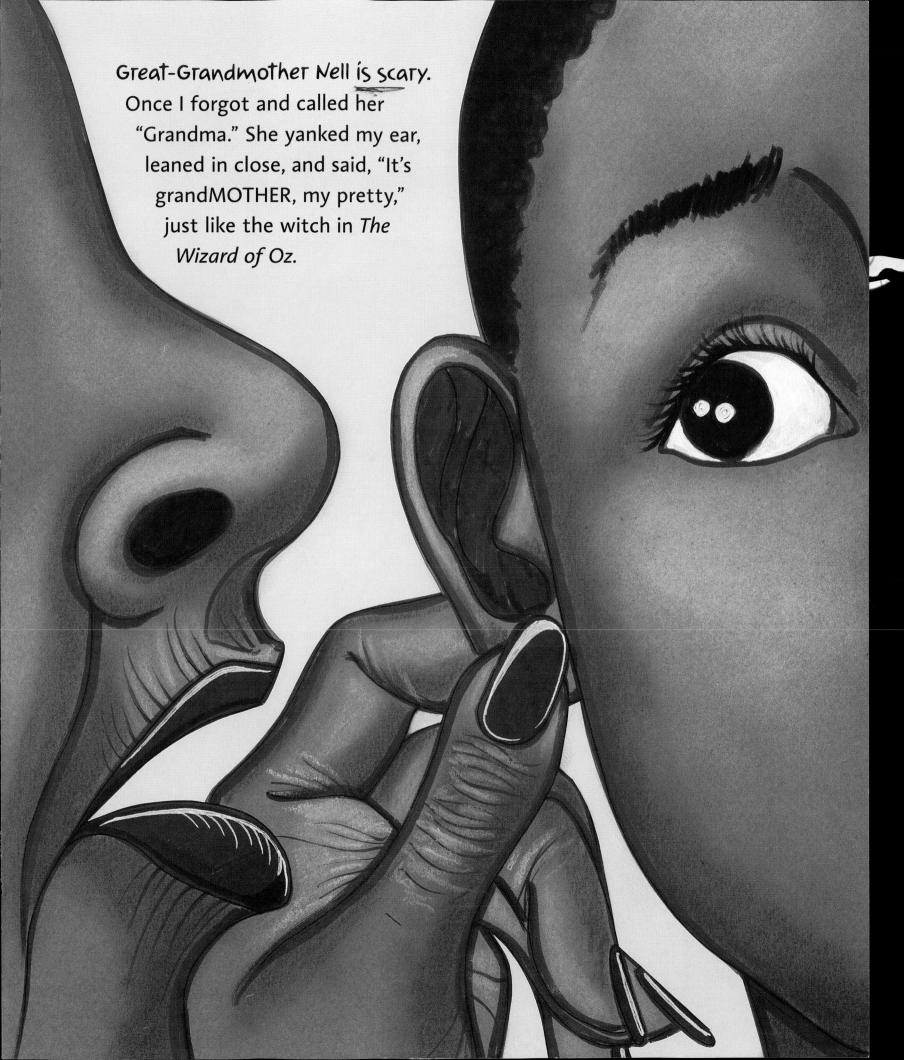

Great-Grandmother Nell is scary. Once I forgot and called her "Grandma." She yanked my ear, leaned in close, and said, "It's grandMOTHER, my pretty," just like the witch in *The Wizard of Oz.*

Great-Grandmother Nell fries fish and boils grits for breakfast.

I like fish, but for breakfast? And with the heads on and the creepy fish eye looking right at me from my plate?

Great-Grandmother Nell likes the beach. When we go, she poses in her bathing suit like she's a movie star. I pretend to be a movie star too, but she clicks her tongue. "Scandalous!" she says, so I stop.

Great-Grandmother Nell has a short, stubby glass with a picture of a spider on one side. She fills the glass with something that looks like apple juice and takes tiny sips. One spider glassful lasts all day.

She let me taste it one time.

"Yuck!" Now I know why she takes tiny sips. "Why do you drink it?" I ask.

"Heart medicine," she says. "Broken heart."

I reach for her, but she turns away.

Great-Grandmother
Nell never hugs.

Great-Grandmother Nell is prickly, but her bedroom isn't. A princess could sleep there. I'm not allowed to play in Great-Grandmother's room, but sometimes she lets me go in, just to look.

A ballerina doll sits in the middle of the bed, her long, cloth arms and legs folded just right. I want to pick the ballerina up, but her expression makes me think she might tell.

Great-Grandmother Nell has a special dresser called a vanity. It has a cushiony stool in front and mirrors all around, even on the shelves.

Great-Grandmother Nell looks in the mirror and growls. Then she turns and growls at me. I squeal and run, hoping she'll chase me. She doesn't.

Great-Grandmother Nell's room smells sweet, like lilacs and roses. Powder puffs and lipsticks and nail polish and wigs and pearls and earrings and bottles and bottles and bottles of perfume crowd the vanity shelves.

Mirrors make it look like there are more bottles than there really are.
All shapes and sizes and colors. Fancy glass, blue and green, pink and
yellow. From New York or London or Paris.

The ones I like best have
sparkly glass tops with stems
that Great-Grandmother
dabs behind her small ears.

"Here," she says and dabs me with something that smells like vanilla.
Then she sniffs me hard and loud with her wide nostrils.

Great-Grandmother Nell is stern, but she is glamorous. Her skin is chocolaty brown, and her lips are painted ruby red. After she puts on lipstick, she presses her mouth to a tissue. She colors my lips too, then shows me her tissue trick. "To make sure you are wearing just enough, but not too much," she explains. I pucker my lips and kiss the air.

Great-Grandmother Nell never kisses.

Great-Grandmother Nell is ninety-six, and she remembers every minute of her life. "All of it, from the day I was born," she tells me.

She remembers when she only had to pay fourteen cents to see a double feature at the movies and a Hershey bar cost a nickel.

She remembers the time her sour cherry pie won first prize at the church picnic and May Ella Carter (who always bragged about her blue-ribbon blueberry pie) was "mad as a hornet."

She remembers the time her best friend said they couldn't be friends anymore because of her brown skin.

"Is that when your heart got broken, Grandmother?" I ask. She looks out the window and whispers, "The first time."

I pat her hand.

She lets me.

I VOTED

I WON'T LIVE WITH JIM CROW

CIVIL RIGHTS CONGRESS

I VOTED

HONOR KING: END RACISM!

HONOR KING: END RACISM!

HONOR KING: END RACISM!

UNION JUSTICE NOW!

BOSTIX EWT0327E

WT0327E ORCH R W 36

ORCH RIGHT

ADMISSION

44.00 24X

R#E0AA72

SECTION/AISLE ROW/BOX SEAT

$44.00

$9.00

CELEBRITY SERIES

ALVIN AILEY

AMERICAN DANCE THEATER

WANG THEATRE

TREMONT ST. BOSTON

2015 8:00 PM

SEC.

ORCH R

MC1740IN

ROW

W

B 44.00

SEAT

36

57343472946

ALVIN AILEY
AMERICAN DANCE THEATRE

50 YEARS

1st

BEST PIE

THE COLORED RIGHT TO VOTE

Papa says Great-Grandmother Nell won't be with us much longer because she is so old.

I don't think he's right.

She's old, but she's not worn out.

Tonight I climb out of bed and sneak into her room. The ballerina is sitting on the vanity stool watching other ballerinas in the mirrors. She won't notice me. A lamp is on by the bed, but Great-Grandmother Nell is sleeping.

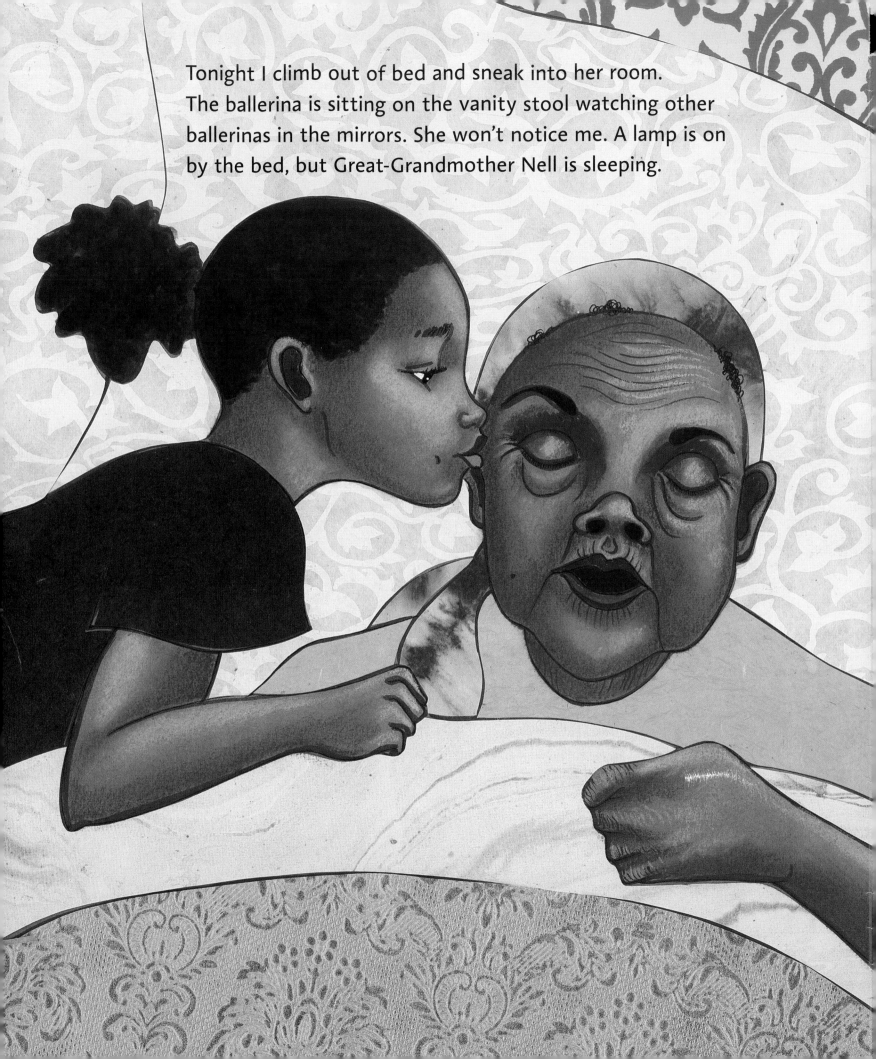

I can tell because she is snoring like a dragon. No fire is coming out, but her nostrils get bigger and smaller every time she breathes.

Even asleep, Great-Grandmother Nell is scary. But I like her that way. I give her a little hug. She smells like peaches.

I kiss my grandma.

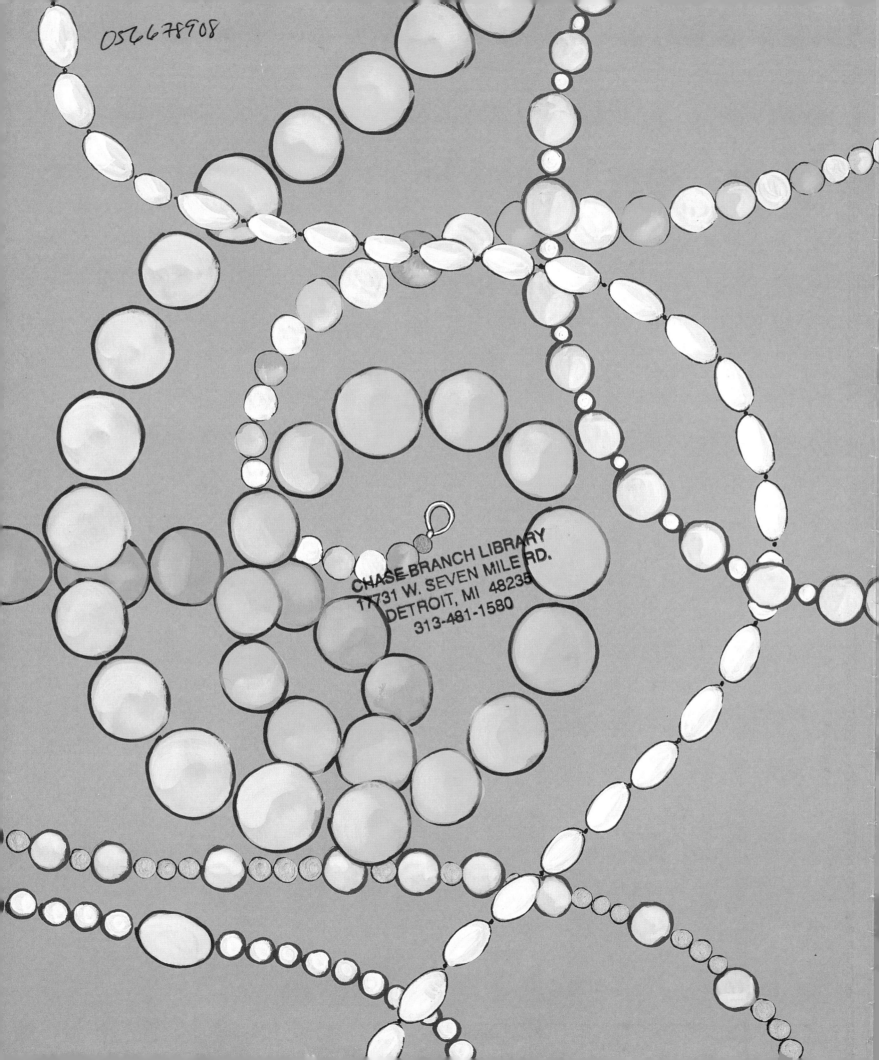